MY MOON WISH.

MY
MOON
WISH

Written and illustrated by
Jane Brown

ISBN: 978-1-941953-92-1

Printed in Canada

Published by:
Butler Books
P.O. Box 7311
Louisville, KY 40257
(502) 897—9393
Fax (502) 897—9797

www.butlerbooks.com

For Ollie

When the moon is bright and the night is still, the Moon Rabbit appears, high on a hill.

He dances all night between shadows and leaves, searching for Moon Wishes left in the trees.

What is your secret wish? Can you share? Hang your wish in a tree. He will find it there!

Moon Rabbit bright, Moon Rabbit fair, take my wish from the tree. Send it high in the air!

As your eyes become weary and close for the day, he will hop by your window to whisk you away.

In the hush of the night, a bright train all aglow will invite you to ride on a moonlit rainbow.

Your Wish Train journey is about to begin. Place your hand on the button. Press GO to begin.

Take a seat in the engine. Sit tight in the light, as the Wish Train flies higher and then out of sight.

You'll fly over houses covered in snow. It gets more exciting the higher you go.

Moon Wishes and secrets flow through the air as the Wish Train rolls onward. Look down if you dare!

As the train passes moonscapes and places brand new, a marshmallow Wish Station comes into view.

Place your wish in its Wish Box,
then close your eyes tight as
you hurtle back homeward,
filled with delight.

Put your head on your pillow.
Look up at the moon.
Wish hard that your Moon Wish
comes true very soon.

As the new morning sun sets the horizon alight, the Moon Rabbit slowly fades out of sight.

Moon Rabbit bright, Moon Rabbit fair, keep my Moon Wishes safe as we whiz through the air.

Fly high with me on a rainbow of light, then bring me back home to my pillow tonight.

Make-A-Wish® is the largest wish-granting charity in the world. Every 34 minutes in the United States and its territories, Make-A-Wish grants a life-changing wish for a child with a critical illness. More than 315,000 wishes have been granted in the U.S. since 1980. More than 450,000 wishes have been granted worldwide. Make-A-Wish serves every community in the United States through 60 chapters.

Make-A-Wish believes when a wish is granted, a child replaces fear with confidence, sadness with joy, and anxiety with hope. Wishes give children the strength to fight their critical illnesses. Research now shows a link between wishes and a child's health and well-being. Wishes are more than just nice; they're a necessary part of a child's treatment plan.

Make-A-Wish needs your help to grant the wish of every eligible child. To learn more about how you can volunteer, donate, and spread the word about its mission, visit: **wish.org**.

Proceeds from the sale of *My Moon Wish* books will be donated to Make-A-Wish.

About the Author

Jane Brown was born and raised in Herefordshire, England, and the idyllic countryside influenced her career as an artist. She has always loved quality children's books and was inspired to write *My Moon Wish* while staying in the small English village of Inkpen.

"I wanted to create a peaceful book that encompassed the mystery of the moon and a child's simple wish," she said.

Jane Brown has lived in Kentucky for more than 25 years. She has two grown sons and one grandson, Ollie.